NODDY AND THE BUNKEY

BY Enid Blyton

CONTENTS

THE WOBBLY MAN WAS CHEERFULLY WOBBLING INTO ALL
THE PUDDLES HE COULD FIND

6

THIS BOOK BELONGS TO

This edition published by HarperCollins Publishers Ltd 1999 for Silverdale Books
An imprint of Bookmart Ltd
Registered Number 2372865
Trading as Bookmart Limited
Desford Rd, Enderby, Leicester, LE9 5AD
First published 1959 by Sampson Lowe
© Darrell Waters Limited 1959 as to all text and illustrations
Enid Blyton's signature mark and the word 'NODDY' are Registered
Trade Marks of Enid Blyton Ltd
All rights reserved
ISBN 0 26 167252-5
Printed and bound in Italy

1. A VERY RAINY DAY

ONE morning Noddy looked out of his window
to see what sort of a day it was. "Raining!" he
said. "Raining and raining! My little car won't like
that. It hates getting muddy."

He dressed himself quickly, and sang a little song.

> "It's raining, it's raining,
> Ploppity-plop.
> I see all the raindrops
> Go hippitty-hop,
> All down my window,
> Pittery-patter,
> It's raining, it's raining,
> But what does it matter?"

7

"Parp-parp!" called the little car from the garage. It liked to hear Noddy singing.

"I'm coming!" said Noddy. "I'm just going to have some breakfast! I shan't be long, because wet days are always busy ones for us! Now, where did I put my breakfast egg? Oh, here it is, in my saucepan!"

After breakfast Noddy put on his mackintosh and went out into the rain. "Goodness—it's pouring!" he said. "I wish you had a hood to put up, little car. My passengers will get very wet! I know —let's pop up to see Big-Ears and borrow his big umbrella."

So away they went to Big-Ears' house. On the way they met Sally Skittle's children splashing off

8

to school, and the Wobbly Man cheerfully wobbling into all the puddles he could find.

"Nice to have no feet on a day like this!" called the Wobbly Man to Noddy. "Can't get them wet in the puddles—ooh, that was a lovely splash, wasn't it?"

Mr Plod, the policeman, was standing in the middle of the road, looking very gloomy. "Hallo,

Mr Plod!" said Noddy, driving up to him. "Nice weather for ducks, isn't it?"

"Don't make silly remarks," said Mr Plod, crossly. "It's just my luck to have to come out this wet morning, because there's going to be a lot of traffic."

"Oh—what traffic?" said Noddy, looking up and down the street. "I can't see anyone at all, except the old Wobbly Man wobbling into another puddle—and Mrs Noah going shopping with some of the animals from the Ark. No wonder she has to have such a big umbrella!"

"Move on, please, Noddy," said Mr Plod. "And just be careful how you go this morning. I tell you there'll be a lot of traffic on this road soon. A circus is moving from Rocking-Horse Town to Bouncing-Ball Village—vans, cages, and goodness knows what!"

"A circus!" said Noddy, delighted. "Oh, I hope I meet it! I wish it were stopping in our town! Which way is it coming, Mr Plod?"

"THERE'S A CLOWN DRIVING THAT VAN!" SAID
NODDY. "HEY, CLOWN!"

11

"Don't bother me," said Mr Plod. "Oh my goodness, here comes Mrs Quack and her family again—for the *third* time this morning! Anyone would think they *liked* the rain."

"Well, they do," said Noddy. "Didn't I tell you it was nice weather for ducks? Hallo, Mrs Quack— you've forgotten your umbrella!"

"Noddy, if you want to be funny, go and be funny somewhere else," said Mr Plod, waving on the happy family of ducks, all pleased to feel the rain-drops trickling down their backs. "And be care-ful—that circus is coming down past Big-Ears' house, through Toadstool Wood—and the road is very narrow there."

"I'll go and meet the circus! I was going to see

Big-Ears anyhow!" said Noddy, and drove off at top speed. He was halfway to Big-Ears' house when he heard the sound of rumbling wheels coming down the woodland road.

"The circus! I'll park my car under a tree and watch it go by! What fun! Oh, bother this rain—it's trickling down my neck!"

It was a good thing Noddy did go under the trees with his car, because the circus vans took up almost all the road as they went by.

"There's a clown driving that van!" said Noddy. "Hey, clown!"

But the clown was wet and miserable and he took no notice.

"Oooh—cages! Are there lions inside?" said

Noddy. But the cages were all closed up because of the rain. Nobody took any notice of Noddy at all. It was very disappointing.

And then, just as the very last van was going by, a door opened at the back of it, and someone tumbled out, howling! The someone landed in the middle of a large puddle, and made an enormous splash.

"Wait for me, wait for me," he yelled at the last van. But on it went, and soon disappeared with the rest of the circus.

Noddy stared at the person who had tumbled out of the van. He had never seen anyone like him before. Whatever was he?

"Hoo-hoo-hoo! Help, help!" howled the strange-looking person. "I think my leg's broken. Help!"

2. BUNKEY

NODDY jumped out of his car and ran up at once. "Who are you?" he said. "You look very peculiar."

"I'm a bunkey," said the odd-looking person. "Surely you have seen a bunkey before? I'm half a monkey and half a bunny. Can't you see my rabbit-ears?"

"Yes," said Noddy, staring. "Good gracious! I didn't know there *was* such a creature. Bunny-ears and a monkey-face—well, well—a *bunkey!* Are you hurt?"

"Yes, I am," said the bunkey. "It's my leg. I fell on it. You look kind. Could you help me, do you think?"

15

"Would you like to get into my car? I could drive after the circus and stop it, and help you back into your van again," said Noddy.

"No! They were very unkind to me at the circus," said Bunkey, big tears rolling down his cheeks, and his bunny-ears waving to and fro. "I never had enough food. I had to do all the heavy work. They didn't even wait to pick me up when I fell out. Nobody wants me there!"

Noddy felt very sorry. He put his arms round

Bunkey and pulled him gently to his feet. "I don't *think* your leg is broken," he said. "Look, get into my car and I'll take you to my friend, Big-Ears — he lives near here. He will give you some buns and hot cocoa, and let you dry your clothes. What a pity you had to fall into such a *big* puddle!"

Bunkey limped to the car and got in. He wore a big straw hat with a floppy brim, and his rabbit-ears went through holes in it, and stuck straight up. He really did look peculiar. He liked Noddy's little car very much.

"Some people are very lucky," he said, as he got in. "Fancy having a car like this. Oooh—my leg does hurt! You are being kind to me. What's your name?"

"Noddy," said Noddy, nodding his head very fast and making his little bell jingle. "Now—hold tight, Bunkey."

And away they went to Big-Ears' house. Noddy hooted as soon as he got there and Big-Ears came to the door. He was most astonished to see Bunkey.

"What's this?" he said, as Noddy helped Bunkey out. "Who is he? Where did you get him from?"

"He's a bunkey," said Noddy. "Haven't you ever heard of one, Big-Ears? I thought you knew everyone and everything!"

Big-Ears stared at Bunkey as if he didn't believe his eyes. "Well! In all my hundred years I have never seen a bunkey before," he said. "Bunny-ears and a monkey-face—well I never! What's he doing in your car?"

Noddy told him, and helped Bunkey into the Toadstool House, holding his arm because Bunkey limped so badly. Big-Ears' cat, Whiskers, was sitting by the fire. He took one look at Bunkey and fled out of the back door, yowling. Bunkey gave an enormous sigh. "It's very hard to be a bunkey," he said. "People either stare or run away."

"Poor Bunkey," said Noddy. "There now—sit down. Can he have something to eat and drink, Big-Ears?"

"Yes," said Big-Ears, and went to get some buns and put milk on to make hot cocoa. Soon the bunkey was gobbling the buns and enjoying himself.

18

SOON THE BUNKEY WAS GOBBLING THE BUNS
AND ENJOYING HIMSELF

19

"Wasn't it unkind of the circus not to stop and pick up poor Bunkey, Big-Ears?" said Noddy. "Big-Ears, could you let him stay here for a day or two till his leg gets better?"

"I'm afraid not," said Big-Ears.

"But why, Big-Ears? You've got plenty of room," said Noddy.

"Er—well—Whiskers wouldn't like it," said Big-Ears.

Bunkey got up at once and limped to the door.

"I won't stay if I frighten your cat," he said, sadly. "Not everyone likes bunkeys, I know. I'll go out into the rain and get soaked. I'll have nowhere to sleep, no home, nothing. But I'll certainly go. Goodbye!"

"No, no Bunkey! I'll help you!" cried Noddy, and ran after him. "You can come and stay at my little House-For-One. I'll look after you till your leg's better. Big-Ears is very, very fond of his cat, he's not really being unkind."

But Bunkey went sadly out into the pouring rain, limping worse than ever. Noddy couldn't bear to see his big rabbit ears flopping down.

"Get into my car again! I'll take you home," he said. "The Tubby Bears will be kind to you—and so will little Tessie Bear. We'll all help you till your leg's better."

"Oh, thank you, thank you!" said Bunkey, and gave Noddy a hug. "No one's ever been so nice to me before. I'll return your kindness, Noddy, really I will!"

21

Soon they were driving through the wood back to Toy Town. Bunkey cheered up at once when he was in the car. "Ooooh—what a *wonderful* car!" he said. "And what a fine driver you are, Noddy!"

Noddy was pleased. He drove rather too fast down the main road, and Mr Plod saw him and shouted at him.

"Hey! Slow down! What do you think you're doing, Noddy? And who in the world is that with you?"

"It's a bunkey!" shouted Noddy, proudly. "He's coming to stay with me."

"A *bunkey*—looked like a monkey with bunny-ears to me," said Mr Plod, staring after them. "Ah yes, of course—bunny and monkey—a *bunkey*. Well, I never! Now where did little Noddy get hold of *him?*"

3. NODDY IS VERY KIND

BUNKEY thought Noddy's house was lovely. He sat down in a chair and looked round it. "Aren't you LUCKY?" he said. "A car of your own—a house of your own—well, well, some people are lucky, like you—and some people are unlucky, like me! Still, you deserve to be lucky, Noddy, you're the nicest little fellow I've ever met."

"Am I really?" said Noddy, pleased, and his head nodded till his bell almost fell off.

"Yes. Quite the nicest. *And* the kindest. *And* the cleverest, too," said Bunkey. "The way you drive that car! I never saw anything like it. That policeman shouldn't have shouted at you like that."

"Oh, Mr Plod — he's *always* shouting at me," said Noddy, taking off his wet mackintosh. "He doesn't think I am a good driver at all."

"If he shouts at you again, I'll go and chase him," said Bunkey, fiercely. "I won't let anyone shout at you."

"Oh well," said Noddy, pleased, "he's not so bad really. Now, take off your wet things and I'll dry them for you. You can wear my dressing-gown till they're ready."

And very soon Bunkey's wet clothes were drying in front of Noddy's fire, and steam rose up and filled the cosy room. Bunkey sat in Noddy's dressing-gown, and talked and talked. He told Noddy such interesting stories about circus life that Noddy felt he could listen all day.

"Let me see your poor leg," said Noddy at last. "I'd forgotten about it. I'll bathe it for you. And you shall sleep in my little bed tonight, and I'll sleep in the armchair."

"Certainly *not*," said Bunkey, at once. "*I* will sleep in the chair. I wouldn't dream of taking your bed. Really, I never met anyone so kind in my life! Wait till my leg gets better and see what I'll do for you! I'll clean your house from top to bottom. I'll cook your dinner. I'll wash and polish your car. I'll weed your garden. I'll do your shopping. I'll . . ."

"Good gracious! You needn't do all *that*," said Noddy, surprised and pleased. "How nice you are, Bunkey. I'm glad I brought you home."

"I'm so very, very grateful," said Bunkey. "I'll help your friends too, Noddy. Just say what you want and I'll try and do it."

Well, Bunkey's leg got better very quickly. By the next day he was walking properly, and looking very cheerful indeed.

"Now you leave all the cleaning to me," he said. "You go out in your car—but let me clean it first."

And dear me, you should have seen how he cleaned that car! It shone so brightly that little Tessie Bear was quite dazzled when she came by. She was very surprised to see Bunkey polishing it.

"Tessie—this is Bunkey," said Noddy, and told her all about him. Bunkey bowed and said how-do-you-do.

"Noddy has been very, very good to me," said Bunkey. "He's so kind—the kindest person in the world."

"I think so too," said Tessie, and gave Bunkey such a nice smile that he liked her straight away.

"IF THERE IS EVER ANYTHING YOU WANT,
JUST TELL ME," SAID BUNKEY

"You're one of Noddy's friends—so if there is ever anything you want, just tell me, and I'll try and do it for you," said Bunkey.

Tessie laughed. "Well, there's nothing I can think of," she said. "Except that I do wish we had a lamp-post outside our house because my Uncle Bear always bumps into the tree by our front gate at night."

"Ha!" said Bunkey, and finished polishing the car's bonnet quite fiercely. Noddy got into the car and Tessie got in too.

"Goodbye, Bunkey—I'll be back for dinner," said Noddy, and drove off.

"I'll have dinner ready!" shouted Bunkey, and went to weed the garden.

28

"He's nice, isn't he?" said Noddy to Tessie.

"Yes, and he says some very kind things about *you*, too," said Tessie. "Poor Bunkey—how awful to be left behind like that—the circus must be miles away by now. Isn't Bunkey a funny name?"

Noddy laughed and began to sing.

"When I saw his rabbit-ears
 I thought he was a bunny,
 But when I spied
   his wriggly tail
 I said, 'Dear me,
   that's funny!'
 Half a bunny,
 Half a monkey,
 What's his name?
 Of course—it's Bunkey!"

"How *do* you think of your songs, Noddy?" said Tessie. "That's a funny one!"

When Noddy got home he was very pleased. His dinner was ready. The house was clean. The garden was weeded. "I've earned a lot of money this morning," said Noddy. "Do let me give you some for all your hard work, Bunkey."

"Certainly *not*," said Bunkey. "You're my friend. I shall do everything for nothing because you've been so kind. There's only one thing I'd like, Noddy. Show me how to drive your car. Please do."

"All right. I'll show you after dinner," said Noddy. So he gave Bunkey a driving lesson after dinner, and dear me, Bunkey learnt very quickly indeed!

"Let me drive around the town," said Bunkey, but Noddy wasn't sure that was a good idea. "Mr Plod might see you and be cross," he said.

"Then let me take a little drive by myself tonight," begged Bunkey. "He won't see me then."

"All right," said Noddy. "Just a very little drive, Bunkey. But please *do* be careful!"

4. ONE THING AFTER ANOTHER!

BUNKEY waited until Noddy was asleep. Then he slipped out of the front door, opened the garage and took out the little car. He was away for half an hour, and then came back as quietly as he went. He put the car away, slipped back into Noddy's house, and settled himself down in the armchair.

"*Dear* Noddy!" murmured Bunkey to himself. "He's fast asleep. How surprised he will be tomorrow!"

Noddy certainly was surprised! At breakfast-time Mr Plod came knocking at the door, looking very angry. "Come in!" called Noddy, and Mr Plod marched in.

"Noddy!" he said. "Do you know anything about four missing lamp-posts?"

31

"Lamp-posts? No, I don't!" said Noddy, astonished. "Where have they gone?"

"That's what *I'd* like to know!" said Mr Plod. "Four of them—all gone! One went from outside Miss Fluffy Cat's gate, and one from outside *my* gate—and we both heard the noise of a car stopping last night."

"Well, it wasn't *my* car," said Noddy. "I didn't take it out at all last night! Go away, Mr Plod."

"Yes, go away!" said Bunkey, standing up and looking very fierce. "I won't have you talking to my friend Noddy like that."

"Good gracious—it's you again," said Mr Plod, staring at Bunkey. "I saw you the other day, didn't I? A bit of a bunny, and a bit of a monkey, aren't you—well, I don't like the monkey bit!"

"And *I* don't like policemen," said Bunkey. "Go away. Noddy's my very best friend."

"I'm not so sure," began Mr Plod in his most serious voice, "and what's more I'm not . . ."

Just then someone came running up the front path. It was little Tessie Bear! "Noddy, Noddy!" she cried. "Do you know, when I woke up this morning, and looked out of my window, I saw FOUR LAMP-POSTS in our front garden! Wherever did . . . Oh, hallo, Mr Plod, I didn't see you!"

"Ha!" said Mr Plod. "So that's where those four lamp-posts went to! I'll just go up to your Uncle Bear's and enquire about this. Lamp-posts can't walk, you know! Noddy—you'll hear from me again!"

And away went Mr Plod, looking really angry.

"Horrid fellow!" said Bunkey, staring after him. "I nearly knocked his helmet off! How DARE he be so cross with you, Noddy? I'll pay him out for this. Yes, I will! Why *shouldn't* dear little Tessie Bear have lamp-posts to light her front garden?"

"Bunkey," said Noddy, suddenly. "Bunkey— surely you—surely you didn't take . . .?"

"I'll go and polish the car for you," said Bunkey, quickly, and ran out to the garage. Noddy looked at Tessie, and suddenly began to laugh.

"Oh! He must have done it," said Noddy. "He must have collected all those lamp-posts in my car last night, Tessie, just to light your front garden and please you because you're my friend. Oh *dear!*"

Mr Tubby Bear looked over the garden wall, and called to Noddy and Tessie. "Mr Plod seems in a bit of a temper," he said. "Hallo—who's this peculiar fellow?"

"It's Bunkey," said Noddy. "He's staying with me."

34

"Noddy's been very kind to me," said Bunkey. "Excuse my not shaking paws with you, they're dirty." And suddenly his tail came round instead, and shook hands with the surprised Mr Tubby. "Noddy's the kindest person I ever met," said Bunkey. "I'd do anything in the world for him. And if you're a friend of Noddy's I'd do anything in the world for you too!"

"Well, that's nice of you," said Mr Tubby. "Look out, Noddy—here comes the Bumpy-Dog!"

And sure enough Bumpy came leaping over the wall and flung himself on Noddy. "Oh don't!" said Noddy, sitting down suddenly in a flower-bed. "I said DON'T! Stop it, Bumpy!"

To everyone's surprise Bunkey picked up a clod of earth and threw it at Bumpy. "Go away!" he shouted. "How dare you attack Noddy. He's my friend! Shoo!"

Bumpy was very surprised indeed. He backed away at once. "Don't throw things at Bumpy!" shouted Noddy, getting up. "He's Tessie's dog— and my friend, too!"

"*Friend?* Knocking you over like that!" said Bunkey, fiercely. "I don't believe it. Wait till I get him!" And he made a leap towards Bumpy.

"Oh Bunkey, stop it!" cried poor Noddy, as a great battle began between Bunkey and the Bumpy-Dog, each trying to corner the other. "Oh my lovely hollyhocks! Oh my big red poppies! Oh my nice little garden seat—it's broken. BUMPY! Come here!"

"COME HERE!" shouted Mr Tubby as well, but Bumpy took not the slightest notice. Who was this peculiar-looking fellow in Noddy's garden? Bumpy didn't like him at all. He did his very best to nip him, but he just couldn't.

At last Noddy caught the angry little dog, and, to Bumpy's great surprise and horror, Noddy was furious. "LOOK at my garden—RUINED!" he said. "You silly, stupid dog! And really, Bunkey, you're just as bad!"

Bumpy went sadly into a corner, and sat down on his tail. Bunkey looked very hurt indeed. "I was only protecting you from that savage dog," he said. "He knocked you down—he was going to bite you. Why didn't that big friend of yours over the wall call him off?"

"I DID!" said Mr Tubby. "But I'm sorry to say that dogs don't usually take any notice of me at all. I wish they did. I'm very fond of them. They don't even follow me like Bumpy follows Noddy. What a terrible to-do this is! Noddy's flowers are spoilt! His garden seat is broken! And I couldn't help him because dogs don't take any notice of me!"

Tessie burst into tears. Then Bunkey began to cry too.

"Tessie, don't cry! I only acted like that because Noddy's my friend. I'm sorry! Please, Noddy, forgive me. I'll put your garden right again. Please, Bumpy, forgive me too—and Mr Tubby, don't think badly of me. I'll do something to show you how sorry I am, I really will!"

"You've been very silly," said Noddy, and that made Bunkey even sadder than ever. "*Look at my garden—it's ruined! And all because of you!*"

5. MR TUBBY HAS A PECULIAR
MORNING

"I'M going out in my car," said Noddy. "I really must earn some money. It's going to cost me a lot to get new flowers, and a new garden seat. I can't *imagine* how Bumpy and Bunkey managed to break it between them. Come along, Tessie, you come with me."

So, leaving an angry Mr Tubby and a miserable Bunkey behind them, they set off in the car. Mr Tubby went indoors, growling about bunkeys who were worse than donkeys and a good deal worse than monkeys. Bunkey looked at the spoilt garden and sighed.

Then he rushed out of the gate at top speed, picking up Noddy's garden spade as he went. Presently he was back again with a load of plants over his shoulder—tall hollyhocks, rose trees, poppies and goodness knows what.

He began to plant them. Then he went off again, and this time, good gracious, he came back with a big garden seat over his shoulder! He set it down and rushed off again.

Back he came with another seat. Dear me, Noddy's garden looked a bit crowded now. "There!" said Bunkey, pleased. "That will show Noddy I'm sorry. Now—what can I do for Mr Tubby?"

He looked over into Mr Tubby's garden. Everything was beautiful there. What about the garden shed? Could he tidy it up, and sweep it out?

In a trice Bunkey was over the wall, and in the shed. No—the shed was spick and span, not a thing out of place. The only dirty thing there was a pair of Mr Tubby's boots.

"I'll clean them for him," thought Bunkey. "I'll take them across to Noddy's, and make them shine as bright as can be!"

He thought of Mr Tubby as he polished away. How sad he had been because dogs didn't like him, and wouldn't follow him when he called them! Bunkey shook his head—then he sat up suddenly.

"*I* could make dogs follow him!" he thought. "Yes, I could. Quick—where's some gravy?"

He looked in Noddy's larder—yes, there was a bowl of gravy, smelling very meaty. Good!

And what did Bunkey do but dip his duster in the gravy and polish Mr Tubby's boots till they smelt deliciously of strong, rich gravy!

"Now, dear Mr Tubby, you will get your wish," said Bunkey, smiling all over his monkey-face. "All the dogs will follow you now."

He put Mr Tubby's boots back in the shed. Then he went and sat on one of the new garden seats and thought of Mr Plod. "He's not nice. He wasn't kind to dear, generous little Noddy," thought Bunkey. "I'll have to think of something to make him sorry he was unkind. And fancy making such a fuss about four old lamp-posts! Well—perhaps four was too many. I wish I'd only taken one for Tessie now."

41

Just then Mr Tubby Bear came out and went into the shed. Bunkey sat up at once. "Good! He's putting on his boots!" he said. "And how surprised he looks to see they are clean. Hey, Mr Tubby—I cleaned your boots for you."

"Oh—well, thanks," said Mr Tubby, surprised. He came to the wall, and stared in astonishment at Noddy's garden. "I *say!* What's been happening? Who's been doing all this planting? WHERE did those garden seats come from?"

"I got them for Noddy because his own seat got broken in the fight," said Bunkey. "Just to show him I'm sorry, you know. And now I'm going to chop up the broken one for firewood. Won't Noddy be pleased?"

"Well—it looks to me as if it could well be mended instead of chopped up," said Mr Tubby. "Thanks for doing my boots. I'm off to the shops now."

And away he went, leaving Bunkey looking for a chopper to chop up the broken seat.

Mr Tubby had a most peculiar morning. First of all he saw a friend of the Bumpy-Dog's, a haughty little poodle, and called to her, quite certain she would turn up her little nose and run away. But she didn't. She stood and sniffed the air a little—

and then she scampered across to Mr Tubby, her little tail wagging fast. She sniffed in delight at his boots.

"Ah—you dear little thing—so you want to be friendly after all!" said Mr Tubby, and patted her. Then up came two more dogs, sniffing eagerly.

They began to lick Mr Tubby's boots, and he was even more surprised.

"Licking my boots! What friendly dogs! Well, well—I must be getting along!" And away he went, feeling very proud to have three dogs following him. Now everyone would see that dogs were fond of him after all!

After a little while two more dogs ran up and smelt the gravy-boots. They darted at the toes, and Mr Tubby fell over. In half a minute there were seven dogs round his feet, snapping and growling at one another, trying to lick at the delicious-smelling boots. Mr Tubby began to feel alarmed. He managed to get up and began to run as fast as he could. All the dogs followed him. People stood and stared at the strange sight, and Miss Fluffy Cat shouted and waved her umbrella. "Go away, dogs!" panted Mr Tubby. "Go *away!* Oh my goodness me, now here comes Bumpy-Dog too!"

Poor Mr Tubby—down the street he went, the dogs chasing him in delight, yapping, howling, frisking all over the road. Mr Tubby began to feel very scared. He saw Mr Plod in the distance, and panted up to him.

"Save me, Mr Plod! These dogs—they're all after my feet. Save me!"

Mr Plod stared at the excited dogs in great astonishment. Bumpy-Dog suddenly ran between his legs—and knocked poor Mr Plod over! He roared at Mr Tubby Bear.

"Go away! Take your horde of dogs with you AT ONCE. You're holding up the traffic. Good gracious me, what with the lamp-posts—and the park seats—and someone taking the park flowers too—I don't know where I am! Bumpy, WILL you stop jumping on my feet? Oh my word, there goes my helmet! Bumpy, bring it back!"

But Bumpy didn't. He raced after the rolling helmet, picked it up, and disappeared at top speed with it in his mouth. Mr Plod groaned.

MR TUBBY RAN AS FAST AS HE COULD. ALL THE DOGS
FOLLOWED HIM

45

"This is a bad dream! It must be. Mr Tubby, if you don't take those dogs away, I shall arrest you. Fancy *you* behaving like this! Has everyone gone mad?"

Parp-parp! Parp-parp! That was Noddy coming along in his car with little Tessie Bear. He was most surprised to see Mr Plod sitting in the road without his helmet, and Mr Tubby Bear climbing a lamp-post to keep about a dozen dogs away from his feet.

"What *is* happening?" said Noddy, putting on his brake. But just then Mr Plod roared so loudly that he hastily took it off again, and drove down the road very quickly indeed.

What a morning!

46

6. BUNKEY REALLY *IS* A MONKEY!

NODDY was even more astonished when he saw his garden. It was full of flowers— hollyhocks, rose-trees—and my word—two new garden seats! NOW what had been happening?

"It's that Bunkey again," said Tessie. "He was sorry he spoilt your garden with the fighting—and oh Noddy, he must have been to the park for those flowers—because those seats are *park* seats. And where is your own little garden seat—the one that got broken?"

"It sounds as if Bunkey is chopping it up," said Noddy. "BUNKEY! What are you doing?"

"Chopping firewood for you, dear Noddy," said Bunkey. "I got you two new seats, so the old one will do nicely for firewood!"

47

"You STOLE those seats from the park!" said Noddy, sternly. "Oh *look*—here's the Bumpy-Dog now—and he's still got Mr Plod's helmet. Drop it, Bumpy, drop it!"

Bumpy dropped it, and Noddy put it on the wall. Bunkey looked at Noddy sadly. "I *asked* the park-keeper who the seats belonged to, and he said they belonged to everybody who came to the park. So I took them for *you*, Noddy—you go to the park sometimes, don't you? You said you'd have to have a new seat—so I got you two. Oh Noddy, I meant to please you. Is there anything else you'd like?"

"Don't be *silly!*" said Noddy. "As if you could get me everything I wanted! I suppose if I said I longed to see the *fire engine* rushing down the road specially for me, you'd be silly enough to get it

48

somehow! I don't think I like you any more, Bunkey. You're a most terrible nuisance. Look— you'd better come along to Mr Plod's with me, and own up about the lamp-posts and park seats—and listen, Bunkey—did you have anything to do with all those dogs chasing after Mr Tubby Bear?"

"Well—I only tried to give him something he said he wanted," said Bunkey, tears dripping down his nose. "Dogs following him, you know—he said they never did,

and he wished they would So I polished his boots with your gravy—so that all the dogs would like the smell!"

"BUNKEY! You *didn't!*" cried Noddy, and Tessie Bear gave a sudden giggle. "Bunkey, you certainly *must* come to the police station with me—you can't go on like this. Bring Mr Plod's helmet with you."

"No!" said Bunkey. But Noddy pulled him out to

49

the car, and pushed him firmly in. Tessie squashed in too, and away they went, Bunkey howling dismally, and Bumpy-Dog racing excitedly behind. They met poor Mr Tubby on the way, still halfway up a lamp-post!

At the police station Noddy and Tessie got out first. Then, in a trice, Bunkey leapt out and disappeared—with the helmet!

"He's mad, quite mad," said Noddy, angrily. "BUNKEY! Where are you? Oh come on, Tessie, we'll go in and tell Mr Plod everything."

Mr Plod was inside, looking for one of his old helmets. He was extremely annoyed. "Sit down, sit down," he said. "What a morning! I've had those lamp-posts put back—and I've . . .but, by the way, where's that dreadful Bunkey?"

"I don't know," said Noddy—and just at that very moment Bunkey walked in. "Where's Mr Plod's helmet?" Noddy asked him.

Bunkey grinned. "It's fetching the fire engine for

"YOU'RE NOT A BUNKEY. THERE ISN'T SUCH A THING!
YOU'RE A *MONKEY!*" GROWLED MR PLOD

51

you," he said.

Mr Plod snorted. He marched over to Bunkey and looked at him fiercely.

"You're not a bunkey. There isn't such a thing! You're a *monkey*, that's what you are, tail and all!"

"But — but he's got bunny-ears," said Noddy.

Mr Plod whipped off Bunkey's floppy hat — and good gracious me, the rabbit-ears came off with it!

"Sewn to the hat!" growled Mr Plod. "NOW look at him—he's a monkey all right. And what's more, he *didn't* fall out of that circus van—he was *thrown* out, because of his tricky mischievous ways! I had a letter about him this morning, warning me not to let him live in our town, and . . ."

Mr Plod suddenly stopped speaking, and began to sniff hard. "The fire's smoking!" he said. "Good gracious, it's simply *belching* out smoke! I can't breathe! JUST LOOK at the smoke! Whatever *can* be happening?"

7. GOODBYE, BUNKEY!

BLACK smoke streamed out of the fireplace, and Mr Plod opened the windows to let it out. Soon the street outside was full of smoke too. Noddy and Tessie threw water on the fire, but that made it smoke all the more.

"The police station's on fire!" yelled someone outside. "Send for the fire engine!"

Mr Plod put his head out of the window and bellowed. "It ISN'T on fire!"

But it was too late. The fire engine had been sent for, and in half a minute it came rumbling at top speed down the street, and stopped outside the police station.

Whooooshy-whooosh! Water came pouring into the room and drenched Mr Plod, Tessie, Noddy and Bunkey. "Hey, stop it, firemen! THERE ISN'T A FIRE!" yelled Mr Plod. He rushed out, and Noddy looked at Bunkey.

"Bunkey, did *you* manage to bring the

fire engine here — because you thought I wanted it?" said Noddy.

Bunkey nodded proudly. "Yes, Noddy. I only did it to please you."

"But HOW did you get it here?" asked Noddy.

"Go outside and look up on the roof," said Bunkey, with a sad little grin. "I climbed up there as soon as I got out of the car. All monkeys can climb, you know. But look how I tore my trousers!"

Noddy ran outside—and there, sitting firmly on top of the chimney, was Mr Plod's helmet! It was keeping in all the smoke that wanted to come out, making it rush back down into the room below, instead of escaping out of the chimney!

"So *that's* how he got the fire engine here," said Noddy, staring. "He knew the helmet would keep in the smoke and make it come out through the window so people would think there was a fire . . ."

"And then someone sent for the fire engine!" said Tessie. "Oh what a mess the water has made! Noddy, let's help poor Mr Plod to clear it up!"

A fireman climbed up to the roof and took the helmet off the chimney. The smoke came out properly then, of course, though the fire was now almost out. Noddy and Tessie found a bucket and some cloths, and began to clean up the smoky room.

Mr Plod was outside sending away the firemen, trying to make them believe that he *hadn't* played a trick on them. "Just WAIT till I get my hands

on that bunkey—no, monkey, I mean," he shouted. "Where is he? Noddy, Tessie, where is he?"

"A monkey did you say?" asked one of the firemen. "Oh, he jumped into that little red and yellow car and drove away just now. I saw him."

"But that's *my* car!" said Noddy. "Oh, how very HORRID of him! My own dear little car! He'll be miles away by now."

"Poor Noddy," said Tessie Bear, and put her arm round him. "Let's go back to your house and wash and I'll make you some tea, then you'll feel better."

So, very sadly, they went to Noddy's house—

56

NODDY AND TESSIE FOUND A BUCKET AND SOME CLOTHS
AND BEGAN TO CLEAN UP THE SMOKY ROOM

and would you believe it — the garage doors were open and there inside was Noddy's little car! "Parp-parp!" it said, happily.

Noddy ran to it at once. "Oh! Bunkey must have put it back! Look, Tessie, there's a note

on the seat. I'll read it to you. Listen. 'Dear Noddy, I had to use your car to escape to your house. I have borrowed some things from your washing-line and Mrs Tubby's washing-line too — an old vest of yours, a pair of old red trousers belonging to Mr Tubby and a duster for a scarf. I'll send them back some day. Did you like the fire engine I got for you? I'm sorry you think I'm bad, I really did try to please everyone. Your loving Bunkey.' "

Tessie and Noddy looked at one another. "He really *was* very naughty, Noddy," said Tessie Bear. "But—but—well, I couldn't help liking him, you know."

"I liked him too," said Noddy. "But oh dear— fancy making the fire engine come out just for me!"

"And gravy-boots for Mr Tubby," said Tessie, with a giggle. "And lamp-posts for me. He was so kind—but he really *was* a monkey!"

"I shall always think of him as Bunkey," said Noddy, shutting the doors. "Come on, Tessie, let's have a nice cosy tea before Mr Plod or Mr Tubby or Bumpy come rushing in on us."

Noddy hummed a little song

as he and Tessie got the tea, and it made Tessie laugh.

> "Gravy-boots and lamp-posts,
> Fire engines and smoke,
> A helmet on a chimney,
> What a crazy joke!
> His ears were like a rabbit's,
> He called himself a Bunkey.
> But oh, would you believe it,
> He really was—a MONKEY!"

Have a nice tea, Noddy and Tessie, and don't worry about Bunkey. He'll soon find another circus, and be happy. But he'll never forget *you*, little Noddy, never!